THE VANISHING VILLAGE

Sarah Dixon

Illustrated by Brenda Haw

Designed by Adrienne Kern

Edited by Karen Dolby

Series Editor: Gaby Waters

Additional designs by Kim Blundell and Stephen Wright

Contents

About this Book

The Vanishing Village is a spooky story about a strange village that mysteriously appears at midnight and vanishes without trace by dawn.

Throughout the book, there are lots of ghostly puzzles and perplexing problems which you must solve in order to understand the next part of the story.

Look at the pictures carefully and watch out for vital clues. Sometimes you will need to flick back through the book to help you find an answer. There are extra clues on page 43 and you can check the answers on pages 44 to 48.

Just turn the page to begin the adventure . . .

Aunt Hetty

Ben

Jay

Jay and Ben set off to explore the moors around the village of Little Snoozing, where they are staying with Aunt Hetty. She has been telling them ghostly tales about the ruined castles, deserted manor houses and ancient standing stones on the moors.

Lost in the Mist

Jay and Ben stumbled through the rough grass, looking for the path back to Little Snoozing. It was dark and a swirling, purple mist surrounded them. They were cold and lost.

Ben spotted the blurred outlines of stones on top of a hill, just visible through the mist ahead. He dug into his rucksack for his map. There was a dull ripping sound and it fell to pieces in his hands.

"We'll never find our way back now," Jay groaned.

SPLASH! She found herself skidding into a pool of icy water. She squelched back to dry land and yanked off her soggy boots. As she tipped out the water, a strange piece of metal fell out of her left boot.

Suddenly a bell tolled in the distance. One, two, three . . . twelve strokes. Was it really midnight? Jay glanced at her watch but it had stopped. At least the mist was beginning to clear. She saw lights glowing in the valley below. Soon she could even make out the outlines of houses in a village.

**Look at Ben's map.
Can you find the village on it?**

Asking for Help

It was very confusing. The village was in Mourne Valley, but nothing was marked on Ben's map. Feeling cold and tired, they decided to go down to the mysterious village and ask for help.

As they walked along the cobbled streets, a tingling sensation crept down their necks. Jay shivered. There was no one around except for a girl and a pig. When Ben asked her how to get to Little Snoozing, she looked puzzled.

"Ask Harold," she said. "He'll help you. He's the innkeeper at The Prancing Piglet. I'd take you there myself, but I'm in a hurry. You can see the inn from here. It's the half-timbered building with the tiled roof, two chimneys and two attic windows."

Jay and Ben stared at the jumble of roof-tops ahead. Which one was the inn?

Can you find the inn?

7

The Prancing Piglet Inn

They clattered down the narrow streets towards the inn. Ben tugged a thick rope next to the door and a bell clanged loudly. Immediately, the door opened and a man peered out.

"Come in," he said, smiling. "I'm Harold, the innkeeper."

They followed Harold into a warm, cheerful room with a roaring log fire.

"We're trying to get back to Little Snoozing," Jay explained. "Aunt Hetty will be worried. Can you help us?"

"It's very late and too dark to set off now," Harold said. "You can stay here. I'll make sure your aunt gets a message."

Just then, a boy the same age as Jay and Ben walked in and gave them a friendly grin.

"Could you find these two a room, Thomas?" asked Harold.

Jay was about to protest, but before she could say a word, she began to feel strangely at home in the inn. She was so warm and comfortable in the large wooden armchair by the fire. It would be a long, tiring journey back in the darkness and mist . . . Of course they should stay! She yawned sleepily.

A Strange Dream?

Ben was digging into a hearty breakfast at The Prancing Piglet and was just about to ask Harold if he could phone Aunt Hetty, when . . . OUCH! He woke up with a jolt. A sharp stone dug into his side. The sun dazzled his eyes. He was outside, back on Bleak Moor. Feeling confused, he shook Jay awake.

"What's happening?" she mumbled, rubbing her eyes. "What are we doing here? Where's Harold and Thomas and the village inn?"

They turned to look down into the valley, but the roof-tops and cobbled streets had vanished. All they could see were trees and more trees. Could they really have imagined it all?

How weird! It seemed so real – the village, the girl with the pig, the inn, Harold's homemade soup, the comfortable bed . . .

As they tramped through the heather towards Little Snoozing, Jay had a vivid flashback. She was lying in her bed at the inn, half-asleep. In front of her stood a shadowy figure who was trying to tell her something.

"But that sounds just like my dream," Ben gasped, when Jay described what she remembered.

They stared at one another in disbelief. They had both had the same dream – identical, except the figure had said different things. In their dreams, the words had seemed strange and jumbled, but as Jay and Ben repeated them, they realized the words made an eerie message.

What is the message?

Spooky Stories

Back in Little Snoozing, Jay spotted Aunt Hetty disappearing into the Greasy Spoon Cafe.

"Aunt Hetty!" Jay cried, running into the cafe.

"I got your message," Aunt Hetty smiled.

So a message HAD been sent... But who had sent it? Harold? But that meant their night in the village was real. But if the village was real, why had it vanished by the morning?

"How strange," Jay muttered.

"What is?" asked Aunt Hetty.

"Everything," said Ben. "The message and the village and Mourne Valley..."

"Oh, Mourne Valley's strange all right," piped up an old man.

And this got everyone started. There seemed to be hundreds of mysteries and eerie tales about Mourne Valley. Ben looked around, then gasped in amazement. Perhaps some of the tales were true!

What has Ben realized?

A Case of Clues

Yawn...

They decided to take Aunt
Hetty's advice and go to the
museum. They slurped down
their milkshakes and set off,
determined to find out more
about the mystery village.

The museum looked dismally
dreary inside. There were no
costumes, no suits of armor and
no model castles.

Jay peered into the dusty glass
cases one by one. There was King
Hengist's stamp collection and the
last will of D. Wisp. How boring
and useless. Then she spotted a
small case tucked away in a dingy
corner.

"There used to be a REAL
village in Mourne Valley," she
exclaimed to Ben, minutes later.
"I've even found out its name."

Ben looked blank.

"Remember the villages on your
map and the picture in the inn?"
she said. "They gave me a clue."

What is the name of the village?

Milk Monitor

The Phantom of Gloome Towers

Silas and Titus - the Wayle Twins

This survey covers all villages in Woldshire
Mme Burstière - Corset Maker to the Gentry - Customers - May 1670

Much Flooding	1
Thunder Magna	2½
Snowe-on-the-Wold	0
Stormy Wether	41
Cloud Magna	-2
Sleet	20
Long Blizzard	49
Wraithe-atte-Mourne	3
Much Plagued	0
Drislington	5

Alice Greville — aged 4

Owners of Potboilers and Sundry Thrillers May 1672

Sleet.	
Drislington.	10
Long Blizzard.	200
Thunder Magna.	3
Much Flooding.	1½
Little Snoozing.	33
Stormy Wether.	6
Cloud Magna.	2¾
Snowe-on-the-Wold.	5

(This survey covers all villages in Woldshire.)

Lucky Wishbone

Shopping List
1 partridge pear
2 call
3 Fr
4

14

Will's picklefork

Sir Waldo Raleigh's Potato Knife

Ebenezer Wayle aged 6

Identity Card
Name ~ Groan
Job ~ Creville's Chef

Family Crests

The Tenant of Wildmoor Hall   Lord Gloome   Lord Howlingale

Sir Gervaise Creville   Will Chill   Abbot of Crumbledown

Identity Card
Name ~ GRUMBLE
Job ~ CREVILLE's butler

Readers of
Witch Magazine
April 1668

1 Much Plagued.
1 Long Blizzard.
0 Drislington.
2 Sleet.
2 Wraithe-atte-Mourne.
1 Much Flooding.
0 Drowne-under-Bleak.
1 Stormy Wether.
4 Little Snoozing.
0 Cloud Magna.
   Snowe-on-the-Wold.
   Thunder Magna.

This list covers all villages in Woldshire.

Lord Gloome and Family at rest 1677

Hovel and Garden
Subscriptions covering all villages
in Woldshire
March 1672

Much Flooding ————— 1
Snowe-on-the-Wold —————
Wraithe-atte-Mourne ————— 2
Cloud Magna ————— 10
Thunder Magna ————— ½
Long Blizzard ————— 6
Little Snoozing ————— 7
Drislington ————— 3
Stormy Wether ————— 0
Sleet ————— 4
————— 0
————— 3
————— 8

Lord Crumhorn
alias Red Arrow-highwayman

Lady Wayle's Beauty Lotion

The Headless Ghost of
Wildmoor
Castle - as seen
by Claire Vayant

Alice's Toy Duck

Cryptic Carvings

Ben was amazed. More than three hundred years ago, there had been a village in Mourne Valley, called Wraithe-atte-Mourne. Then suddenly the village had vanished. But how?

As Ben wandered away from the case, he spotted something interesting across the room. He barged past some yawning tourists to take a closer look. It was a sundial from Wraithe-atte-Mourne. Its base was decorated with strange carvings.

"What are they?" Jay asked.

"They're words written in Sombric Script," said the curator, coming up behind them.

She handed them an old book and added, "There's a chapter on Sombric Script in here. It should help you work out what the carvings say".

Ben impatiently flicked through the book. Perhaps the sundial would tell them more about Wraithe.

Can you work out what the carvings say?

16

16th century Sundial
from Wraithe-atte-Mourne donated by Dawn Korus

Herbert's wine-making kit

Otto's odds & ends pot

interesting specimen of

Pots of fun for eve...

Mug pieces found near Little Snoozing by B. Kerr in 1850

The Mug People

The Mugs lived in Mourne Valley thousands of years ago. They were named after their custom of burying their dead with brightly-colored mugs and ample supplies of coffee and drinking chocolate to keep them awake during their journey to the underworld.

The Mugs are famous for the standing stones on Sombre Hill (sometimes wrongly called a stone circle). The arrangement of the stones appears jumbled, but they are in fact arranged in 14 rows, running north to south. Each row contains between two and seven stones, and there are large gaps between some of them. There are also four single stones which stand alone in the group. The very famous UFO specialist, Don Vannikin, claims these rows are landing markers for ancient extra-terrestrials and are still regularly used as a refuelling point.

The Mugs told many stories and carved them onto disused standing stones in Sombric Script. In 1888 Sir Diggory Fyndes translated their famous saga, Bare Wilf, from Sombric Script, using his Grid Principle. There are no gaps between words in Sombric Script and numbers are written as upright strokes – 1 is one, 11 is two, etc.

The Sombric Alphabet

Later, back at Aunt Hetty's cottage, Jay and Ben planned their next move. The carvings on the sundial were useless rubbish. They had nothing to do with the vanishing village at all!

Jay thought about what the man with the newspaper had said in the cafe. Today was the 30th of April. If the legend was true, that meant tonight was the last time the village would appear this year.

"Let's go back to Mourne Valley tonight and see," she said.

Ben remembered the last words of the cloaked figure, urging them to return. Where would they find an object from the village to take with them?

"The only thing we've seen is that rotten sundial," he sighed. "We can't take that!"

He looked at Jay glumly, then nearly fell off his chair in amazement. Out of the corner of his eye, he caught sight of an object that looked suspiciously like something he had seen in the village inn.

What has Ben spotted?

19

Midnight Meeting

T hat night, Jay and Ben scrambled through the heather to the pool on the top of Bleak Moor, clutching the silver spoon. In the distance a bell tolled twelve times.

Their hearts pounded as they gazed at Mourne Valley below. Would the village appear again?

"Look!" Ben cried. "Lights... and houses!"

He raced down towards the village with Jay panting behind him. A familiar tingling sensation ran down their necks when they reached the first cottages in the valley.

A maze of winding streets led them past more cottages and a bell tower to a small village square and a river with stepping stones. Jay leapt onto the first stone, then...

"Over here!" hissed a voice.

SPLASH! Jay lost her balance and found herself knee-deep in icy water again. A cloaked figure holding a lantern stood in front of her. It was the person they had seen last night.

"Come with me," the figure said. "We must talk."

Ben hesitated. Who was this mysterious hooded character and what did he want?

Suddenly, Ben caught sight of the figure's face, lit for an instant by the glow from the lantern. He grinned. So that's who it was.

Who is the mysterious figure?

An Eerie Tale

They followed Thomas along an alley and into The Prancing Piglet Inn. Jay pulled off her wet boots and soggy socks, and all three sat down in front of the blazing fire.

"I'm so glad you've come back!" Thomas exclaimed. "The amulet must be found. It's all Creville's fault. We're trapped. We can't do anything. So I had to get you back to release us from the curse. I'm sure the amulet's in Gloome Towers..."

"Hang on!" Jay said, confused. "What's the amulet? Who's Creville? What's he done?"

"And what's this curse?" Ben gulped, feeling uneasy.

The room fell silent. Outside, the wind began to howl. Ben shivered. Thomas threw another log on the fire, then he leaned forward and began to tell them an eerie tale.

Creville dabbled in science and sorcery. At night, luminous mists hung over Creville Manor and sinister wails echoed around its grounds as he carried out his mysterious experiments.

The local lord of the manor was called Sir Gervaise Creville. He owned our village of Wraithe-atte-Mourne.

Creville always needed money to buy peculiar things like unicorns' horns, griffins' tongues and dragons' teeth for his weird experiments, so he sold our crops and animals, leaving us short of food.

Things went from bad to worse and finally we went to Creville to beg him to give us food, or we would starve. We peered through the locked gates of Creville Manor.

The next day, the Dragon Amulet, our magic charm, had disappeared from the ancient statue in the village square. Next to the statue lay Creville's ring. He had stolen the amulet to use in experiments because it has strange powers...

Suddenly there was a flash of purple light. Seconds later, Creville's dogs hurled themselves against the gates, growling ferociously. We fled back to the village.

The amulet protects the village from harm. It is made of an unknown gold metal, shaped like a dragon. No one knows where it came from, but it has always been kept in the statue. According to legend, the village vanishes if the amulet is taken away...

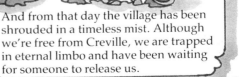

And from that day the village has been shrouded in a timeless mist. Although we're free from Creville, we are trapped in eternal limbo and have been waiting for someone to release us.

23

The Search Begins

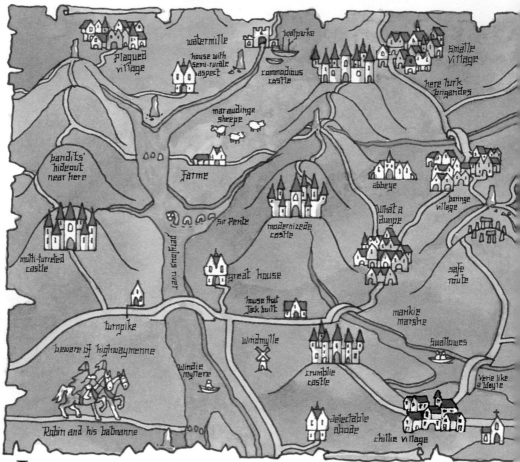

Plagued village

watermille

house with semi-rurale aspect

boatparke

commodious castle

smalle village

here lurk brigandes

maraudinge sheepe

bandits' hideout near here

farme

abbeye

boringe village

Sir Pente

modernizede castle

What a dumpe

multi-turreted castle

perylous river

safe route

great house

house that Jack built

mankie marshe

turnpike

windmylle

swallowes

beware of highwaymenne

windie mynere

crumblie castle

Vere like a Wayte

Robin and his batmanne

delectable abode

chillie village

J ay and Ben stared at Thomas, aghast. It was a terrible story. But what could they do to help?

"We need you to find the Dragon Amulet and bring it back to the statue," Thomas explained. "Only then will the village be released from limbo."

"But how are we going to find the amulet?" Jay cried. "It could be anywhere!"

"All we know is that Creville stole it," Thomas said. "He probably took it to his secret laboratory in Red Arrow's cell, hidden deep in the dungeons of Gloome Towers.

"But that was over 300 years ago!" exclaimed Ben. "It won't be there now."

"How do you know?" Thomas asked.

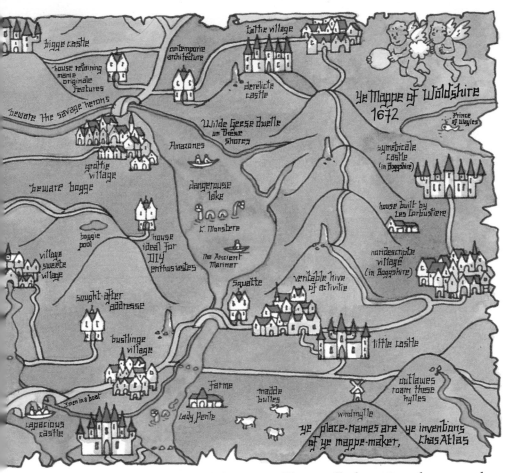

Inside the map:

bigge castle

contemporie architecture

tattie village

house retaining manie originale features

derelicte castle

Ye Mappe of Woldshire 1672

Prince of Wayles

beware the savage herons

Wilde Geese dwelle on these shores

Amazones

symebicale castle (in Boggshire)

grottie village

dangerouse lake

K. Monsbere

house built by les Corbustiere

beware bogge

boggie pool

house ideal for DIY enthusiastes

The Ancient Mariner

nondescripte village (in Boggshire)

village sweete village

sought-after addresse

Squatte

veritable hive of activitie

bustlinge village

3 men in a boat

Farme

madde bulles

little castle

outlawes roam these hylles

rapacious castle

Lady Pente

windmylle

ye place-names are ye inventions of ye mappe-maker, Chas Atlas

---

Jay and Ben looked doubtful. It WAS their only lead . . .

"But how do we get back to the village? Tomorrow is the 1st of May," Jay said.

"The village is always here, even if you can't see it," Thomas replied. "When you return to Mourne Valley with the amulet, go to the site of the statue. Then the curse will be lifted."

He unrolled a tattered map and added, "You can see Gloome Towers on here. It's the castle with six turrets."

"That map's ancient," Jay said. "We need to find Gloome Towers on our modern map . . . if it still exists."

Can you find Gloome Towers on Ben's map?
What is the shortest route there?

The Perplexing Plan

J ay clattered along the cobbled lane out of the village. Ben hurried after her. As he ran past the last houses, he felt the same sharp tingle in his neck that he had noticed before.

Gasping for breath, they scrambled up the steep hill to Bleak Moor. When they reached the top, they looked down into Mourne Valley for one last glimpse of the village.

Suddenly, Ben pointed and cried out in amazement. Even as they watched, the valley was growing darker and mistier... the village was vanishing in front of their very eyes!

They raced on across Bleak Moor, leaving Mourne Valley behind, shrouded in darkness. Before long, a ruined castle loomed above them, sinister in the moonlight. This was Gloome Towers, but only one of its six turrets was standing.

Would they still be able to find a way into the dungeons? Jay stared at the heavy turret door. It looked very solid and locked. She grabbed its rusty handle and began to heave and tug. Suddenly the door swung open, sending her flying.

Nervously, Ben peered inside. As his eyes became used to the dark, he could see hundreds of stone steps leading down into the blackness below. On the back of the door hung a tattered piece of parchment. It was a plan of the cells with prisoners' names written on it.

But where was Red Arrow's cell? Ben scanned the plan again and again. Just as he was about to give up hope, a name suddenly caught his eye. Hadn't he seen it in the museum?

Where is Red Arrow's cell? How can they get there?

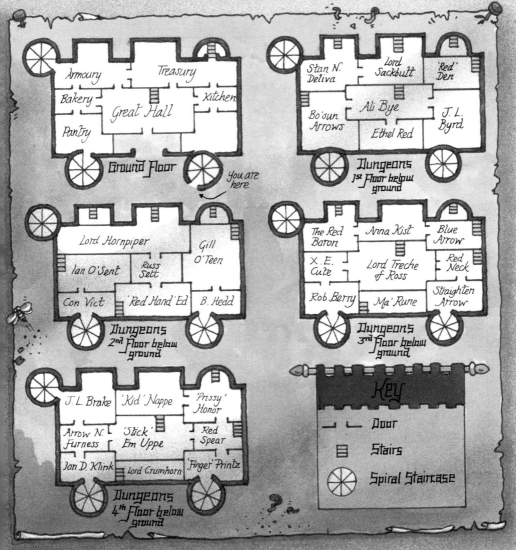

Armoury Treasury
Bakery Great Hall Kitchen
Pantry
Ground Floor
You are here

Stan N. Deliva | Lord Sackbutt | 'Red' Den
Bo'sun Arrows | Ali Bye | J. L. Byrd
Ethel Red
Dungeons
1st Floor below ground

Lord Hornpiper | Gill O'Teen
Ian O'Sent | Russ Selt
Con Vict | 'Red Hand' Ed | B. Hedd
Dungeons
2nd Floor below ground

The Red Baron | Anna Kist | Blue Arrow
X. E. Cute | Lord Treche of Ross | Red Neck
Rob Berry | Ma' Rune | Straighten Arrow
Dungeons
3rd Floor below ground

J. L. Brake | 'Kid' Nappe | 'Prissy' Honor
Arrow N. Furness | 'Stick' Em Uppe | Red Spear
Jan D. Klink | lord Crumhorn | 'Finger' Printz
Dungeons
4th Floor below ground

Key

⌐ ⌐ Door

▤ Stairs

⊛ Spiral Staircase

27

Down in the Dungeons

THUD

They crept gingerly down the steps to the dungeons. Ben shone his torch into the first cell. It looked empty, so he marched confidently inside. Suddenly the air was filled with beating wings and high-pitched squeals.

"Bats!" he shuddered.

They raced into the next cell and down a flight of steps. They ran on through silent, spooky rooms and stumbled up and down slippery stone stairs until they reached Red Arrow's cell.

Jay shivered. The cell was very creepy. Huge cobwebs hung from the ceiling and everything was covered in a thick layer of dust. Now their search for the amulet began. They peered in pots, crawled under the table and looked in gaps in the wall. But as they had feared, it was nowhere to be found.

A gust of wind whistled through the dingy dungeons. Was that laughter? Jay caught her breath, listening hard. An eerie silence followed. Perhaps she was imagining things.

THUD! The sound came from above. Alarmed, Jay and Ben sprinted back up to the turret door. It had jammed shut. They tugged and heaved as hard as they could, but the door wouldn't budge. They looked at one another in horror.

"Come on," said Ben, trying to sound calm. "Let's try to find another way out."

They raced back down to the dungeons and through a maze of cells. Soon Jay felt completely lost. Perhaps they would never find a way out. They could be trapped for ever in the damp, dark dungeons.

Ben shone his torch ahead but could only see a dead end. There was no way out. He slumped miserably against the wall. With a loud CLICK, a lever sprang shut beneath his right foot. The next second, the wall disappeared and Ben found himself falling backwards. He had discovered another tunnel.

Feeling more hopeful, they followed the passage into a dank room. High above, Ben could see sky. They were at the bottom of a dried-up well.

"We can climb out of here using those ropes and ladders," he said.

Jay was less sure. The ladders had rungs missing and the ropes were old and frayed. But it was their only chance of escape.

Can you find a safe route to the top of the well?

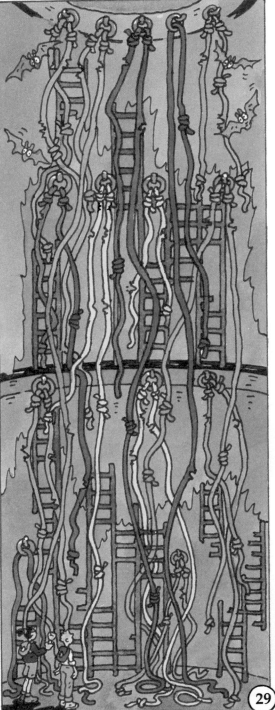

The Deserted House

Jay and Ben clambered out of the well and looked around. They were in the grounds of an old deserted manor house. As Ben gazed up at its sightless windows, he had a strange feeling that someone was watching him. Was that a shadowy figure slipping out of view?

"There's something creepy about this house," he shivered. "Let's get out of here."

"Wait a minute!" hissed Jay.

She stared at a pile of broken statues and crumbling stones in front of the house. The symbols on some of the pieces of stone looked familiar. Then it came to her in a flash. She remembered where she had seen those symbols before and knew where she was.

Where are Jay and Ben?

Cracking Creville's Code

Perhaps the Dragon Amulet was hidden inside Creville Manor. Hundreds of years had passed since Creville lived there. Thomas had said nothing about it being there, but . . .

"We could have a look, just in case," Jay said, as they nervously crept towards the house.

The door creaked open and they stepped inside. When their eyes grew used to the gloom, they realized they were in a large hall.

Jay wandered past the suits of armor, faded tapestries and pewter pots. Then she spotted a book lying on a wooden chest by the window.

Mond aywh atis itli keto brav elin ofly
ingm achi newh aldo esth emoo ntas teti
keiw antt ofin dout ifon tyic ould live long
enou ghfo rimc erta inth atth eans wers
will befo undi nthe futu reTu
esda yiha rede cide dtof inda wayo fliv
ingf orev erto dayi trie d67e xper imen
tsas reco mmen dedi nold merl insb ooko
fope llsn oneo fthe mwor keda ndmy usel
esss erva ntsg rumb lean dgro anha
vebu rnltm ysup pera gain
Wedn esda ythe book ofsp ells tell
soft heam azin gpow erso fthe drag
onam ulet iamg oing tost eali tand
seew hati tcan dofo rmeT
hurs dayw hata disa ppoi ntme ntth eamu
leti sjus talu mpof powe rles smet alih
aved ecid edto thro wawa ythe spel
lboo kand buya noth eron ell3
Opmi veju stma cleou tthe scra wled foot
note curs esth eamu leto nlyh aspo wers
D

tohe lpth alwr etch edvi llag eifi
cant uset heam ulet noon eels eisg
oing tous eiff
nda ytee heew hata shoc ktho sevi llag
ersw illh avew hent heys eeth atth
eirp reci ousa mule thas gone andt heyl
lnev erfi ndit iveb roke nthe amul etin
twoa ndhi dden onep iece unde rthe
king ston eint hest onec ircl eihu rled
theo ther also mesh eepo nthe moor
smay thev illa gers alll ivem iser ably
ever afte rSat
urda yive foun dawa ytol ivef orev eron
tyon evit alin gred ient wasm issi ngCu
rses itsw orke dbut imay have done some
thin gsli ghtl ywro ngim here fore verb
utst ucki nmyh omi dbro wncl oaka ndev
enwo rsei seem toha vebr ough tgro anan
dgru mble with meno wthe ynev erle
avem ysid ehow ihat ethe sigh toft
hema trea dyaa argh

If this diary dares to roam, box its ears and send it home to Sir G. Creville

As she blew away the thick layers of dust from its cover, the book fell open at a page covered with spidery writing. But the words made no sense.

"It's Creville's diary," she said, reading the bookmark.

"It might tell us something useful, if we could read it," said Ben, looking over her shoulder.

They stared at the page, baffled. Then Ben realized the writing was in a simple code. Slowly, he began to work out what it said.

BANG! A door slammed somewhere upstairs. An icy draft crept into the hall. Were those footsteps?

Jay and Ben did not stay to find out. They dashed out of the house, across the garden, through the open gates and on into Mourne Valley.

"I know what's happened to the amulet," Ben panted, as he ran. "We've got to go to the stone circle."

What does the diary say?

The King Stone

Soon they were scrambling up the steep hill towards the stone circle. Now they had to find the King Stone and one half of the Dragon Amulet.

Jay stared at the ancient stones. There seemed to be hundreds of them. Some were still upright, while others had toppled over, but there was nothing to show which one was the King Stone.

"This is hopeless," Ben groaned.

"I wonder if the stones have any words or carvings on them," Jay suggested. "Like the . . ."

She stopped, struck by a sudden idea. Of course! The writing on the sundial. They already knew how to find the King Stone.

**The pictures show opposite sides of the big arch in the middle of the stone circle, looking in opposite directions.
Can you spot the King Stone?**

The Missing Piece

As soon as they found the King Stone, they began to dig, using sharp pieces of flint and stone. Seconds later, Ben held an oddly-shaped piece of metal in his hand . . . it was half of the amulet.

Jay stared at the piece of amulet, puzzled. It reminded her of something she had seen before. But what? Then she remembered. The first night, lost on the moor . . . the strange metal object in her soggy boot . . .

"I've already found the other half!" she exclaimed.

She fumbled in her rucksack. It HAD to be there. Frantically, she pulled everything out, then gave the bag a last desperate shake. But the amulet had gone.

What could have happened to it? She racked her brains, but it was no use. There was nothing she could do. The missing piece could be anywhere. Now the vanishing village would remain trapped in limbo for ever.

In gloomy silence, they trudged miserably back to Little Snoozing. As she shuffled along the high street, Jay gazed glumly into the shop windows. Garden gnomes, tartan socks, cuddly toys, huge sticks of Little Snoozing rock and . . .

The missing half of the amulet! She stared open-mouthed in disbelief.

Where is the missing piece of the amulet?
How did it get there?

37

Returning the Amulet

The shopkeeper remembered them from the cafe and gave the piece of amulet back to Jay.

"I thought it was just an old brooch," he smiled. "Ideal for my window display."

"There's no time to lose!" Ben exclaimed, speeding out of the shop. "We've got to get back to Mourne Valley."

When they reached the valley, they found the woods where the village should have been.

"But Wraithe IS still here," said Jay, ducking under a low branch. "We just can't see it."

It was strange to think that they were walking down invisible streets past houses and people. Somewhere among the trees was the site of the statue.

Suddenly Ben heard the sound of rushing water. He pushed through some bushes into a small clearing.

"I'm sure this is the river which ran through the village square," he said. "We must be near the right place now."

The trees by the river looked very old. Ben thought he had seen some of them before.

This gave him an idea. He began drawing imaginary lines between trees and boulders.

"I know where the statue is," he yelled. "Follow me!"

Where should the statue be?

What Happened Next

Clutching the two halves of the Dragon Amulet, they rushed to the spot where the lines met . . . A sharp tingle ran down their necks. The ground shook beneath their feet. In the distance, a bell began to toll. Each stroke sounded nearer and nearer. A clock struck twelve . . .

Jay and Ben blinked, then stared, dazed. They were in a bustling village square. A boy waved as he walked towards them. He looked very familiar.

"What's happened?" Ben gasped. "Who are you?"

"Tom, you idiot," the boy said, puzzled. "Don't you remember?"

"Where are we?" Ben asked.

"In Wraith-at-Mourne, of course," Tom laughed.

"But that's impossible!" Ben exclaimed.

"Why?" said a voice.

Ben turned and saw Aunt Hetty sitting at her easel, smiling at them. As he glanced at the shops around the square, he gaped in disbelief. Wraith was a modern village! It was as if the village had never vanished. But that was impossible – or was it? Could they have changed the course of history when they returned with the amulet?

But where was the amulet? It had disappeared! Had someone stolen it? Would the village vanish again? Jay wandered around for a while, feeling anxious.

Then she smiled. She knew the amulet was safe.

Where is the amulet?

The Three Strangers

Later that day, Tom climbed the steep path to Bleak Moor with Jay and Ben trailing behind. They were off to explore the ruined castle on Wildmoor Hill, which was haunted by a headless woman in green.

"You two are acting very strangely," Tom said. "What's the matter?"

Jay tried to explain about the vanishing village, the amulet and the curse, but Tom just thought it was a good story.

As they reached the top of the moor, Ben spotted three people a little way ahead. He nudged Jay. Hadn't they seen them before?

As the figures came closer, Jay and Ben saw their faces clearly for the first time. They gasped...

Then Jay chuckled. She knew who the three strangers were. And she guessed they weren't too pleased. Nothing had worked out quite as they planned.

Who are the three strangers?